The Three Little Gators

Helen Ketteman

Illustrated by
Will Terry

Albert Whitman & Company, Morton Grove, Illinois

For Connor, Patrick, Lucy Anne, and Joop with love,
from Great-Auntie Helen.—H.K.

For Zack, Aaron, and Seth.—W.T.

Library of Congress Cataloging-in-Publication Data

Ketteman, Helen.
The three little gators / by Helen Ketteman ; illustrated by Will Terry.
p. cm.
Summary: In this adaptation of the traditional folktale, three little gators each build their house
in an east Texas swamp, hoping for protection from the Big-bottomed Boar.
ISBN 978-0-8075-7824-7
[1. Folklore.] I. Terry, Will, 1966- ill. II. Three little pigs. English. III. Title.
PZ8.1.K54Th 2009   398.2—dc22 [E] 2008028085

The design is by Carol Gildar.

For more information about Albert Whitman & Company, visit our web site at www.albertwhitman.com.

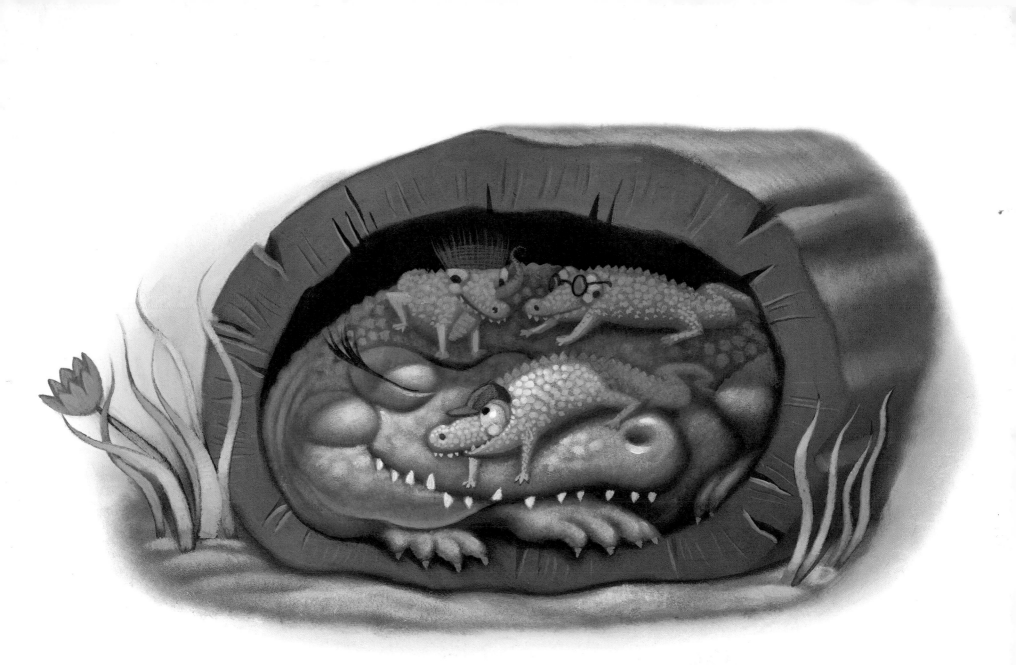

Once, three little gators lived with their mama in an east Texas swamp.

One day, Mama said, "It's time you young 'uns set out on your own. Make sure you build houses strong enough to keep you safe from Big-bottomed Boar. Tasty, tender gators are his favorite snack."

So the three little gators set off.

Soon, they came upon some rocks. "Aha!" said First Gator.
"A house of rocks would be safe from Big-bottomed Boar."
"Bad choice," said Second Gator. "Rocks are heavy and too much work."

"*Way* too much work," said Third Gator.
"Heavy or not, I'll build my house with rocks." First Gator began rolling rocks into a pile. His brothers waved good-bye and walked on, until . . .

Plonk! A stick landed on Second Gator's head.

He looked up. In the tree above him, Hawk was building a nest. "Aha! I'll build a stick house. That will be easier."

"Bad choice," said Third Gator. "It's still too much work."

Third Gator waved good-bye and walked on, until . . .

Sloosh! Third Gator came to a river. He stopped to rest on the soft, damp sand along the riverbank. "Aha! A house of sand would be the easiest one to build," he said.

He pushed the sand into a big pile and dug a tunnel. Then he made a door from branches.

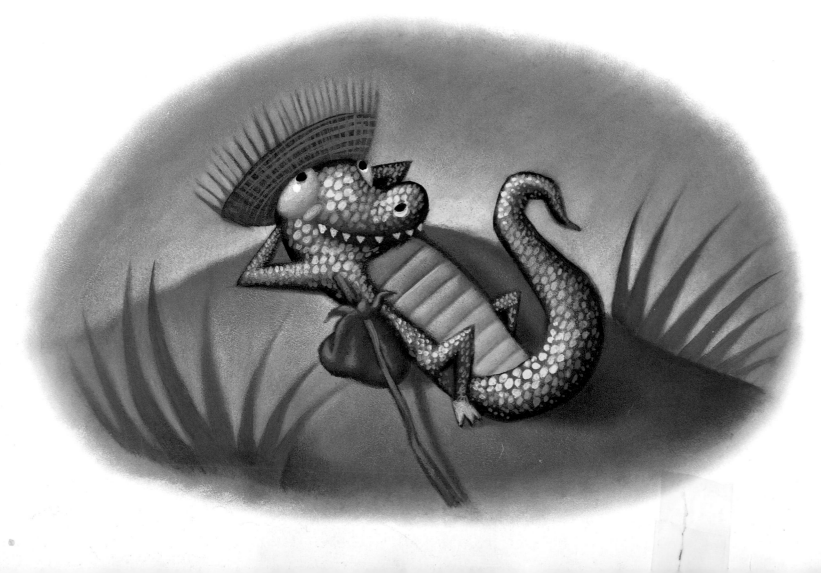

"Ha!" Third Gator laughed. "Big-bottomed Boar won't even know this is a house." And with that, he crawled in and fell asleep.

After a while, Third Gator was awakened by a loud noise.
Snurf, snurf! Snort, snort!
"Little gator, let me in. I smell tender gator skin."

Third Gator trembled inside his house, but he called back,
"Go away, Big-bottomed Boar! I'll never open up my door!"

"Then I'll wiggle my rump with a bump, bump, bump and smash your house!" Big-bottomed Boar wiggled his bottom and bumped it against Third Gator's house.

Sand flew everywhere.

Third Gator ran faster than a fox after a muskrat. He scrambled through the brambles to Second Gator's house.

But it wasn't long before the two little gators heard a loud noise.
Snurf, snurf! Snort, snort!
"Little gators, let me in. I smell *two* tender gator skins.
Chasing you has made me thinner. I need two little gators for my dinner!"

The two little gators shivered at the sound of Big-bottomed Boar's raspy voice, but they answered, "Go away, Big-bottomed Boar! We'll never open up the door!"

"Then I'll wiggle my rump with a **bump, bump, bump** and smash your house!" answered Big-bottomed Boar.

He wiggled his bottom and
bumpity-bumped it
against Second Gator's house.
Sticks flew everywhere.

Second Gator and Third Gator raced faster than snakes after a bullfrog. They rushed through the brush to First Gator's house.

But it wasn't long before the three little gators heard a loud noise.

Snurf, snurf! Snort, snort!

"Little gators, let me in.

I smell *three* tender gator skins.

Chasing you has made me thinner.

I need **three** little gators for
   my dinner."

The three little gators shook at the sound of Big-bottomed Boar's terrible voice, but they called back, "We'll never open up the door! Go away, Big-bottomed Boar!"

"Then I'll wiggle my rump with a **bump, bump, bump** and smash your house!" answered Big-bottomed Boar. He wiggled and bumped, and waggled and thumped, but he could not smash First Gator's house.

"I'll get you yet!" Big-bottomed Boar snorted. He climbed on the roof and squeezed into the chimney. He grunted and wheezed and snorted and sneezed as he inched his way down.

But the three little gators were ready for him. "Bad choice!" they called.

When Big-bottomed Boar finally dropped out of the chimney, he landed right on the hot grate of First Gator's barbecue grill.

Grill stripes burned into his big bottom, and Big-bottomed
Boar raced out of the house faster than a thunderbolt!

Then Second Gator and Third Gator went outside and began piling up rocks.

"Good choice!" said First Gator, and he helped them build strong houses.

And Big-bottomed Boar never bumped his big, striped rump their way again.

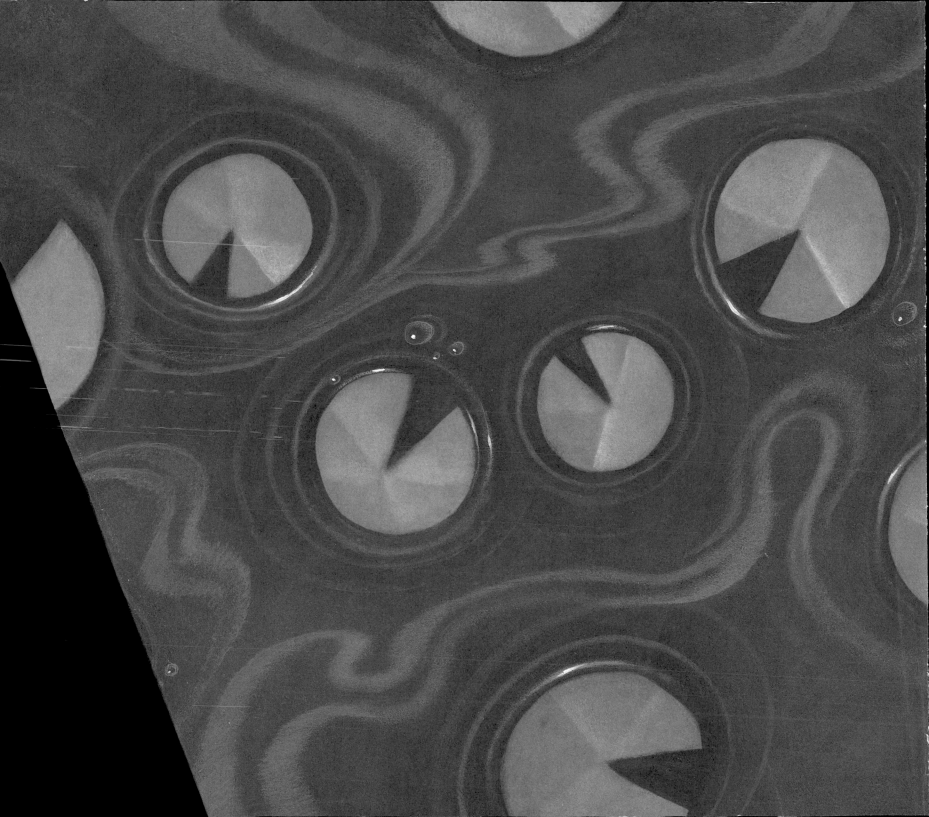